KU-428-985

THIS BOOK

BELONGS TO:

DUDLEY SCHOOLS LIBRARY
AND INFORMATION SERVICE

Schools Library and Information Services

S00000671741

For my best friend and publisher,
Klaus Flugge

JUDLEY PUBLIC LIBRARIES

L 47991

671741   SCH

JY MCK

Copyright © 2004 by David McKee.

This paperback edition first published in 2005 by Andersen Press Ltd.

The rights of David McKee to be identified as the author and illustrator of this work
have been asserted by him in accordance with the Copyright, Designs and Patents Act, 1988.

First published in Great Britain in 2004 by Andersen Press Ltd., 20 Vauxhall Bridge Road, London SW1V 2SA.

Published in Australia by Random House Australia Pty., 20 Alfred Street, Milsons Point, Sydney, NSW 2061.

All rights reserved. Colour separated in Switzerland by Photolitho AG, Zürich.

Printed and bound in Italy by Grafiche AZ, Verona.

10   9   8   7   6   5   4   3   2   1

British Library Cataloguing in Publication Data available.

ISBN 1 84270 468 0

This book has been printed on acid-free paper

THE CONQUERORS

David McKee

Andersen Press
London

There was once a large country that was ruled by a General.
The people believed that their way of life was the best.
They had a very strong army, and they had the cannon.

From time to time the General would take his army and attack a nearby country.
"It's for their own good," he said. "So they can be like us."

The other countries resisted – but, in the end,
they were always conquered.

Eventually the General ruled all the countries except one . . .
This was such a small country that the General had never
bothered to invade it. But now it was the only one left.
So one day the General and his army set out again.

The small country surprised the General.
It had no army and offered no resistance.
Instead, the people greeted the soldiers as if they were welcome guests.
The General installed himself in the most comfortable house
while the soldiers lodged with families.

Each morning the General paraded his soldiers and then wrote letters home
to his wife and son.
The soldiers talked with the people, played their games, listened to their stories,
joined in their songs, and laughed at their jokes.

The food was different from their own.
They watched it being prepared, then ate it. It was delicious.
With nothing else to do, the soldiers helped the people with their work.

When the General realised what was happening, he was furious.
He sent the soldiers home . . .

. . . and replaced them with fresh ones.

But the new soldiers behaved just as the others had. The General realised that he didn't need a large army there. He decided to return home and leave just a few soldiers to occupy the country.

Once the General was gone, those soldiers hung up their uniforms and joined in the daily life.

The General returned home triumphant, with his soldiers
chanting as usual:

"We are the conquerors.
We are the conquerors."

He was glad to be back, although somehow it was different. The cooking smelt of the cooking of the little country. People were playing games from the little country. Even some clothes were those of the little country. He smiled and thought: "Ah! The spoils of war."

That night, when he put his son to bed,
his son asked him to sing to him.
So he sang the only songs he could remember.
The songs of the little country –
the little country he had conquered.

Other books by David McKee

Elmer

Three Monsters

Not Now, Bernard

Mr Benn - Gladiator

Who is Mrs Green

Zebra's Hiccups